THE LIBRARY OF
# EMERGENCY PREPAREDNESS™

# BLACKOUTS
## A PRACTICAL SURVIVAL GUIDE

Ann Byers

rosen
central™

The Rosen Publishing Group, Inc., New York

Published in 2006 by The Rosen Publishing Group, Inc.
29 East 21st Street, New York, NY 10010

**Library of Congress Cataloging-in-Publication Data**

Byers, Ann.
Blackouts: a practical survival guide / Ann Byers.
    p. cm.—(The library of emergency preparedness)
Includes bibliographical references and index.
ISBN 1-4042-0535-7 (library binding)
1. Emergency management—United States—Juvenile literature. 2. Electric power failures—United States—Juvenile literature.
I. Title. II. Series.
HV551.3.B94 2006
613.6'9—dc22

                                                                    2005014292

*Manufactured in Malaysia.*

**On the cover:** Only the lights from vehicles shone brightly in New York City during the August 14, 2003, blackout.

# CONTENTS

# Introduction

There was nothing unusual about this Thursday in New York City. It had been a normal day at work and Amy was on her way home. She was in the last car of the subway train. The car was crowded; about twenty people had to stand.

Without warning, the train stopped. The air conditioning quit. Then a voice came over the loudspeaker: "Attention, passengers, we have lost power." It was 4:10 PM on August 14, 2003.

Amy wondered, had something happened to the subway line? Was the whole city without electricity? Maybe something was wrong with just her train. It would be hours before she learned the truth: she was in the middle of the largest power outage in North American history.

At first, everyone on Amy's train stayed calm. But fifty minutes after the subway stopped, the lights suddenly went out. It was coal black and people started screaming. They were trapped, in the dark, in a tunnel under the ground. The lights came back on in a few seconds, but many passengers were now frightened. Some were crying. Sometime later, the car's doors finally opened.

When she stepped out of the train, Amy was not on the subway platform. She was in an 18-inch (45.7-centimeter) space between the tunnel's wall and the car. Policemen were holding flashlights so the passengers could find the

During the August 14, 2003, blackout in the northeastern United States, many commuters who rely on trains to travel to and from New York City for work found themselves stranded in the city. Commuters, who had slept on the steps of the General Post Office in Manhattan, are pictured here on the morning of August 15.

ladders to the platform. When she finally reached the sunlight, she checked her watch. It was 6:10 PM. She had been locked in the subway car for two hours.

And still her ordeal was not over. She was one of the luckier New Yorkers. She did not live far from where the subway stopped. But when she got home, she discovered that nothing worked. Her home phones were dead without electricity. Her cell phone was not getting a signal. She could not use her television or radio to find out what had happened—they were both electric. Her clock radio was missing its backup battery, and she did not have a spare.

This is an early-morning view from New Jersey of a New York City neighborhood the morning of August 15, 2003. The blackout began at 4:11 PM eastern standard time the previous day, and affected more than 50 million people throughout the Northeast and Canada.

Not sure how long the power would be out, Amy checked her flashlight. The batteries were dead. Frantically, she pulled out her emergency kit. She had put the kit together after all the talk began about terrorism. But she had not put it together well. The only thing in it that was helpful was cash. She had stuffed one- and five-dollar bills in the otherwise useless kit.

Quickly, before the sun set, Amy headed for a store. She found the streets packed with people on the same mission for food and a telephone that did not require electricity. But most of the stores had closed their doors. She managed to buy an old-fashioned phone and a bag of ice. At least she might be able to keep some of the food in her refrigerator from spoiling.

Then she detected a welcome aroma. The owner of a pizza restaurant had brought out a big barbecue. He was cooking chicken, hamburgers, and ribs to sell to his neighbors.

Fortunately, the sun did not set that late-summer day until almost 8:00 PM. By then, Amy was back at home, with a full stomach, eager for sleep. Her electricity did not come on until late the next day.

# 1 --- Who Turned Out the Lights?

**W**hat Amy experienced was a blackout—a complete loss of electrical power. A blackout can be caused by a storm, an accident, or a problem in the electrical system. It can also be caused by high demand: people using more electricity than power companies can supply.

When demand is high, power companies try to prevent a blackout from happening. They do this by cutting back on the power they release. This lets them save power for the times it is needed the most. Utility companies can reduce power in two ways: a brownout and a rolling blackout.

A brownout is a reduction not in the amount of power, but in the strength of the power. The power supplier lowers the voltage of the electricity. This forces appliances to use fewer watts. It would be like replacing a 60-watt lightbulb with a 40-watt lightbulb. Appliances would still work, but they would not operate as powerfully.

In a rolling blackout, the companies shut off power to certain parts of a city, a few at a time, for a limited period of time. It is a controlled blackout that "rolls" from place to place. Usually, rolling blackouts are scheduled for the times when people and businesses use the most energy.

These strategies, however, are not always enough to prevent a blackout.

A man shops in a darkened store in San Francisco, California, during a statewide rolling blackout that was ordered on March 19, 2001, due to an energy crisis. Hospitals and other emergency facilities operate on a separate grid that is spared from intentional blackouts of this kind.

A blackout can affect a few blocks or several states. It can last for minutes, hours, or days. A blackout might cause only minor inconveniences for some people, like the 2003 North American blackout did for Amy. Or it might be disastrous.

The reason blackouts are so serious is that we depend on electricity. We need electrical power to cook our food, clean our clothes, and wake us up in the morning. We use it to power our tools, light our homes, and place our fast-food orders. At one time, we did all these things without electricity, but we would hardly think of doing them manually today. We even have electric guitars, electric razors, and electric pencil sharpeners.

Even those appliances that are powered by natural gas often will not work without electricity. Some require electronic ignitions to get the gas started. Others use fans or other electric parts. Clothes dryers, home heating units, and other major gas appliances will not work without electric power.

Entire cities run on electricity. Traffic lights, rapid transit, gas pumps—all are electrical. Elevators, cash registers, and security systems run on electricity, too. Computers, televisions, and business machines must all be plugged in to a source of electricity. Even wireless devices, such as cordless and cellular phones, rely on electricity. Indeed, power disruptions can wreak havoc in a city.

The disruption often does not last long enough to cause major damage. Hospitals, airports, and other critical businesses have generators that can supply electricity for a period of time. But an extended blackout poses health and safety problems. Water is pumped from the ground, piped into homes, and purified all by electricity. In a long blackout, water is not available and sewers back up. Communication is slowed and police and firefighters cannot respond quickly. People become frustrated, and crime rises. Fortunately, most blackouts do not last long and are not very widespread.

## Major Blackouts

However, dramatic blackouts have struck large portions of the United States four times. The first was the great Northeast blackout in November 1965. That event blanketed seven states and a large part of Ontario, Canada. It affected

Commuters trapped in a train for nearly eight hours make their way from the railroad tracks on November 10, 1965. This blackout led to the establishment of energy reliability councils to monitor information, create standards, and coordinate power providers.

25 million people. Power was out for thirteen and a half hours.

Because it was sudden and had not happened before, the blackout was very scary. In New York City, 10,000 people were trapped in powerless trains in dark subway tunnels. Others were caught in elevators or stuck in traffic. But people adjusted. Some spent the night in their offices. Others slept in train stations or hotel lobbies. They worked together to make the best of the situation. Ordinary citizens jumped out of their cars and directed traffic. They helped firefighters and police officers rescue people from the subway tunnels. The 1965 blackout was a shock and a hardship, but it brought people together.

The 1977 event was another story. It was a much smaller blackout, limited to New York City and its 9 million people. But it lasted twice as long—twenty-six hours in some neighborhoods. It unleashed a torrent of crime and destruction. For some time, people in the city had been frustrated by social and economic problems. When the lights went out on July 13, some New Yorkers vented their

A wave of crime accompanied the July 13, 1977, New York City blackout. Here, looters take advantage of a smashed store window at an A&P supermarket. Fires were often set to stores after lootings. More than 3,400 people were arrested, and 558 police officers were injured in attempting to restore order.

anger. They smashed store windows and stole whatever they could carry. They set more than 1,000 buildings on fire. The *New York Times* called it a "night of terror."

The largest blackout in the West was much calmer. It occurred during daylight hours and lasted no more than nine hours. Occurring on a very hot day in August 1996, it shut down air conditioners in nine states and parts of Canada and Mexico. Residents of Los Angeles, California, could not go to the beach to get relief from the heat. The power outage somehow triggered a water treatment plant to release 6 million gallons (23 million liters) of sewage onto the beaches. The West Coast blackout affected 7.5 million people.

By far the most serious U.S. power failure was the North American blackout of August 14, 2003. It began near Cleveland, Ohio, and spread within an hour to 40 million people in Ohio, Michigan, Pennsylvania, New York, Vermont, Massachusetts, Connecticut, New Jersey, and 10 million in Canada. Some areas were still blacked out two days later. Parts of Ontario, Canada, were still blacked out for more than a week after power was restored elsewhere.

Because it lasted so long and affected so many cities, the 2003 outage caused serious problems. Water pumping stations were without electricity, so some places did not have drinking water. After the power was restored, people had to boil their water to make it safe for drinking. At least one

## 💡 Major U.S. Blackouts 💡

| Date | Area Affected | Number of People Affected | Duration |
|---|---|---|---|
| November 9–10, 1965 | Northeast states and Canada | 25 million | 13 hours |
| July 13–14, 1977 | New York City | 9 million | 26 hours |
| August 10, 1996 | West Coast from Canada to Mexico | 7.5 million | 9 hours |
| August 14, 2003 | Northeast, northern Midwest, and Canada | 50 million | 5 hours to more than one week |

person died in one of the thousands of fires started during the blackout. Three major airports did not have power, and 400 flights had to be canceled.

## How Blackouts Happen

These blackouts were large and dramatic, but there have been many more. The *Washington Post* reported on August 10, 2004, that "every four months the United States experiences a blackout large enough to darken a half-million homes." How do so many power failures happen? And how do they affect so many?

They happen because one small part of a giant power system fails. They spread because our power systems are connected to one another.

The United States is dotted with more than 6,000 plants that generate electrical power. Nearly half a million miles (more than 800,000 kilometers) of transmission cables carry the electricity from the power plants to homes and businesses. All the parts of this system make up three main power grids. The production and flow of electricity in the grids are monitored by control centers.

In each grid, power generated in one plant can be sent wherever it is needed. What the grid cannot do is store electricity. So the plants try to produce only the amount of power that is actually needed. Energy experts know when demand for power will be high and when it will be low. They rev up production for periods of peak demand, when the most energy is needed.

This system usually works well. When one part of the system has a problem, the other parts can take over for it.

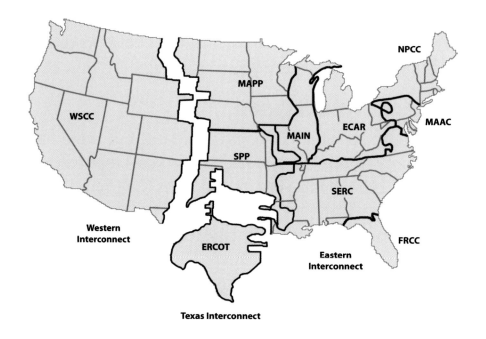

The United States is divided into three main power grids: the Western Interconnect, the Texas Interconnect, and the Eastern Interconnect. These power grids in turn are made up of ten North American Electric Reliability Council (NERC) regions that monitor the electrical activity within each area.

If one plant needs to be shut down for repair, other plants take up the slack. If a transmission line fails, its load is shifted to another line.

The trouble comes if a problem occurs when the entire system is operating at full speed. When all the power plants that are online are producing all the power they can and all the transmission cables are humming at top capacity, a disaster can result if something goes wrong. The working plants and lines cannot handle the added load. Sometimes they will disconnect themselves from the grid so they will not be overloaded and fail, too. Then even more demand is placed on the remaining parts of the system. They either disconnect also or fail themselves. The different parts of the grid go out like dominoes, one after the other. This is called a cascading effect because the outages tumble like a cascading waterfall.

A cascading blackout that darkens millions of homes can begin with a very small problem in the system. In 1965, a single relay in one power line caused four more lines to fail in fewer than three seconds. Lightning triggered

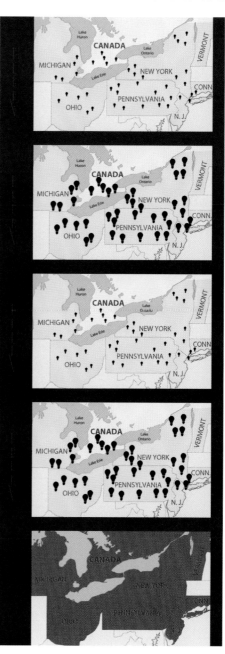

This frame-by-frame depiction illustrates the cascading blackout that affected the Northeast region of the United States in 2003 between 4:10 and 4:13 PM. The lightbulbs on the map indicate the locations of power plants that initially tried to accommodate the surge that happened in Ohio, but then automatically disconnected from the grid, nearly simultaneously, in a sixty-second period starting at 4:10. The cascading effect resulted in a complete blackout by 4:13.

the New York City blackout of 1977. The 1996 West Coast and 2003 North American blackouts started when power lines sagged into trees and were short-circuited.

Unlike some other disasters, blackouts are completely unpredictable. The only thing that can be said for certain is that they will occur. It is, therefore, important to be ready.

# 2 --- Just in Case

**Y**ou probably do not need to prepare for every possible disaster. Not everyone has a significant chance of being in a flood, a hurricane, or a tornado. However, anyone can be in a sudden blackout. Therefore, everyone needs to be ready.

Being ready for a blackout takes planning. You will want to do two types of planning. First, you should have a family communication plan so you are not worried about others in your family. Second, you need a contingency plan. A contingency is anything that might happen. In a contingency plan, you prepare for anything and everything you think is possible.

## Communication Plan

When disasters strike, families are not always together. You need a plan for keeping in touch with your family. Decide where you will meet if you cannot get to your home. Ask a friend or relative who lives out of state to be your family contact person. Make sure everyone knows the name and phone number of that person. When any major emergency takes place, everyone can contact that person as soon as possible.

You also should know how to get hold of emergency services. You do not dial 911 for every emergency. You should dial 911 only for events in which lives are in danger. Keep telephone numbers of police and fire departments, your utility company, and your local hospital in an easily accessible place.

## Contingency Plan

Planning for any disaster means thinking through what might happen and how you can cope with those possibilities. In a blackout, the most obvious probability is that none of your appliances will work. You need to plan how you would function without those conveniences. Let's consider

A New York City police officer directs traffic in one of the famous intersections of the world—Times Square—during the 2003 blackout. Cars moved along cautiously as workers poured into the streets. During a blackout, pedestrians should be extra alert, and drivers should treat intersections as if they were four-way stops.

a likely scenario, from coming home from work or school in the afternoon to going to bed at night. How would that day be different during a blackout? Can you do something now to make your life easier if the worst were to happen?

Start with your ride home. Do you use public transportation? Certain vehicles, such as trams and subways, will not work without electricity. Those that do may be held up by nonworking traffic signals. You may not be able to get home very easily. Think about safe places along your route where you could stay for a few hours if you cannot get home. Is there a friend or relative who lives along your route? Is there a workplace of a family member or family friend at which you could stay? Perhaps there is a recreation center or a store or business where there are lots of people. You will be safer if you are not alone.

If you travel by car, a blackout can be a major problem if you are unprepared. Gasoline pumps operate on electricity, so in a blackout you will probably not be able to fill up your tank. The way to be prepared is to always keep the tank at least half full. Remember, blackouts strike without warning.

When you get home, do you use an automatic garage door opener or an electronic security gate? Some people enter their houses through the garage instead of the front door. An automatic door will not open in a blackout. Prepare now by learning how to use the manual release lever. You may still have difficulty raising the heavy door. It is a good idea to carry a house key or have one in your car just in case.

If you live in an apartment, there should be an emergency plan that is specific for your building. If your building owner or landlord has not provided one, then it is important to create one! Do you rely on an elevator to access the floor where your apartment is located? Be familiar with all the accessible stairways in your building. Find out if they are lit with emergency lighting and if you need an additional key to access them or the floor to your apartment.

What if you arrive home at night and everything is dark? For just such an emergency, you need to have a battery-powered light handy. It needs to be easy to get to. The batteries must be fresh. Just in case the outage lasts for a long time, you should have extra batteries.

Once inside, you will need to have communication with people outside your home. Cordless telephones will not work without electricity, but standard telephones that do not plug into an outlet will. Cell phones may not work either. Sometimes power to cellular antennae is knocked out and your cell phone will not receive signals. Sometimes, so many people are trying to place calls that the system is overloaded. Part of being prepared is having at least one standard telephone.

A standard telephone only has to be connected to the phone jack in the wall to work. Keep a standard phone plugged in to a second jack in your home, or be sure to have it handy as a substitute.

If you are ever in a blackout, you will want to know what is happening around you. The blackout may be part of a larger problem, and police or firefighters may be giving warnings or instructions. Yet televisions and radios will not operate. Make sure you have a battery-powered radio. Don't forget you need enough good batteries to run it.

By this time in our scenario, you are probably hungry. If your stove is electric, you will not be able to cook. You could possibly use a gas stove. You might have access to a gas grill or barbecue outside of your home. You should always have a supply of ready-to-eat food for emergencies such as this. You may also have a problem with water. Water is pumped into homes, and pumps require electricity. So in an extended power outage, water may not be available. Plan now to always have at least 3 gallons (11.4 l) of water in your home for each person living there. Three gallons (11.4 l) should last for three days.

In a power outage, food in your refrigerator can get warm and spoil. If you plan ahead, you might be able to keep this from happening. You can use any extra space in your freezer to make ice blocks. Just fill plastic containers with water. When you fill the containers, leave about an inch of space because water expands as it freezes. Ice stays cold longer than empty air. So, while your refrigerator is without

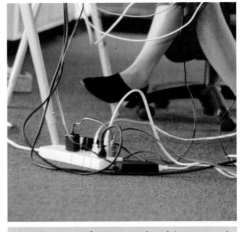

The disarray of wires under this woman's desk all lead into a surge protector. This device protects electronic equipment from surges, sags, and spikes that can accompany the restoration of power.

power, the ice blocks you previously made help keep your food cold longer.

A blackout emergency plan should include protection for sensitive equipment such as computers. When power goes out, or when it surges back on, computers can be damaged. Plan for this possibility by using a surge protector for your computers, monitors, printers, scanners, and other electronic devices. Turn them off when they are not being used. Be careful to shut them down properly each time. It is also a good idea to make backup copies of all important systems, programs, and information stored on your computers.

## Special Needs

People with disabilities or other special needs may depend on electricity more than others. Some have wheelchairs or scooters that use electricity to charge their batteries. Some have life-support equipment, such as breathing machines, that requires electric power. These people should make sure their utility company has their names and addresses on file. Many utility providers keep lists of customers whose lives depend on having electric power. In an emergency, the utility company can locate these customers, get generators to them, or get them to places that do have power. People with special needs should contact the customer service representative of their local utility company any time they move to a new home.

Anyone who relies on a wheelchair or other equipment with a motor should always have a reserve battery—just in case power is lost and the main battery cannot be recharged. Another alternative is to have a manual wheelchair that can be used if necessary. Those on respirators, ventilators, or other forms of life support need to make a habit of fully charging the batteries every day.

People with visual impairments may not be concerned about the dark, but they will need to know how long the power is out. This will affect whether their food is safe to eat. The visually disabled should have a windup or battery-powered clock they can read. It may be braille, talking, or one that can be read by touch.

According to the American Red Cross, a car battery can also be used to restore power to a motorized wheelchair. However, this will not power the chair as long as a wheelchair's deep-cycle battery.

The hearing impaired will not be able to get emergency information delivered on the radio. They may want to have small, battery-powered television sets. Emergency information is usually given not only verbally, but also in American Sign Language or in words scrolled across the screen.

## Emergency Supplies

In addition to a plan, you need an emergency supply kit. An emergency kit for a blackout requires less than the kit for other types of disasters. In other disasters, people face

# PREPARING FOR A BLACKOUT CHECKLIST

### Always

✓ Keep a flashlight and portable radio handy.

✓ Keep a noncordless standard phone on hand.

✓ Keep a supply of water and nonperishable food.

✓ Keep critical medical equipment fully charged.

### Weekly (at least)

✓ Back up computer files.

✓ Fill car's gas tank.

### Twice a Year

✓ Check batteries for freshness.

✓ Replace stored water and food with fresh supplies.

### Blackout Emergency Kit

✓ flashlight

✓ battery-powered radio

✓ extra batteries

✓ three-day supply of food with nonelectric can opener

✓ three-day supply of water

✓ cash

the possibility of having to leave their homes. In a black-out, most people can stay home (if they can get there) and wait it out. To be ready for a power outage, you need only a few items.

A flashlight is an absolute must. If the flashlight is not used very much, the batteries should be removed but kept nearby. Batteries inside a flashlight can corrode and leak, damaging the light. Candles may look nice, but they are dangerous. Many of the 3,000 fires reported in New York in the 2003 blackout were started by candles.

A battery-powered radio is also necessary. This will keep you informed about the event and any helpful warnings

A well-stocked, well-organized first-aid kit is essential for any home. Always keep a fresh supply of medications (antibiotic creams, antihistamines, aspirin) and have a compartment for wound cleansing, wound dressing, and hardware such as scissors and tweezers.

and instructions. You may also want to have a battery-powered or windup clock.

An emergency preparedness kit should also have extra batteries. This is in case the original batteries are weak or the outage lasts for a long time. The batteries should have expiration, or "use-by," dates on the packaging. Make sure they are still good.

Perhaps the most important items in a blackout emergency kit are food and water. You should have enough to last three days. The longest blackouts are usually over within three days. Canned meat and tuna will provide protein. Peanut butter will also provide protein. Canned fruit and vegetables will supply vitamins. Granola bars, crackers, and dried foods are easy to store and eat. Don't forget to pack a can opener.

You can buy bottled water for your kit or prepare your own from your tap. Water does not have to be refrigerated if it is treated. For your emergency kit, pour water into clean plastic containers and add four drops of bleach to each quart (1 l). Use plain bleach, not the scented kind. Seal the containers tightly.

Bottled water comes in many varieties in convenient bottles to carry. Whether you buy bottled water or prepare tap water for your blackout kit, store your supply in a dark, cool place away from sunlight.

You should keep your warm clothes and blankets where you can get to them easily. If a blackout occurs during very cold weather, you may need the extra layers of warmth.

Lastly, it is a good idea to put some cash in your emergency kit. If you find you need to buy something, stores may not be able to process checks or ATM and credit card transactions.

These are the items you need in case of a blackout. Keep these supplies together, perhaps in a large plastic bin, backpack, or duffel bag that is easy to find and carry. For a complete disaster preparedness kit, ready for any emergency, you also need first-aid supplies. These items may include bandages, alcohol cleansing pads, antibiotic ointment, and aspirin, to name a few. If you do not include these items in your kit, make sure you know where to find them in your home.

After the emergency kit is assembled, you must check it regularly. Batteries expire. Food, even canned food, does not keep forever. So twice a year—maybe at the same time you change the batteries in your household smoke detectors— check your kit. Make sure the batteries are still good. See if the flashlight and radio still work. Replace the food and water with fresh supplies.

Making a plan and keeping an emergency supply kit probably seem like a lot of trouble. You might never use your plan or your kit. But if you are one of the millions of Americans who has experienced a blackout, even a brief one, you will be glad you were prepared.

# 3 --- In the Dark

**P**icture yourself at home on a summer evening. You have just answered your e-mail and are sitting down to watch a movie. You set the fan on high. Popcorn is popping in the microwave. Then, just as the movie is getting good, everything stops. The fan quits humming. The computer is silent. The television screen goes blank. The room is dark. Everything is strangely quiet.

You wonder if something has happened to your house or if the problem is larger. You look outside. Everything there is dark, too. No house lights, no street lights. This could be a minor power disruption; the electricity could be back on in minutes. Or it could be a blackout that lasts for hours or even days.

What do you do?

## Basics

As with any emergency, the first step is to make sure you and any others are safe. Unless you are near electrical lines that have fallen, you are probably not in physical danger in a blackout. Being trapped in elevators or unfamiliar buildings may be scary, but it is generally not dangerous (see the sidebar on page 31). Keeping calm is probably the most important thing you can do.

These stranded commuters seem to be remaining calm as they gather on a sidewalk after being evacuated from Grand Central Station in New York City during the 2003 North American blackout. As daily routines halted, people cooperated with one another and made the best of a bad situation.

Your next concern is to safeguard yourself and your surroundings from what might happen when the electricity comes back on. Usually the power surges on. That is, it comes on suddenly and strongly. This can damage sensitive electronic equipment such as computers and televisions. It can also short out motors in washers, dryers, air conditioners, and other large appliances.

So you need to turn off or unplug whatever was on before the outage. Especially make sure you turn off anything that produces heat, like stoves and irons. When they come back on, they could overheat and cause a fire if no one is paying attention. Do not, however, unplug your refrigerator, freezer, or furnace. If your house has a water pump, do not shut it off. Turn off everything else except one light. Leaving one light on will let you know when the power is back.

After you have turned everything off, you will want to implement your emergency plan. The first step in that plan is to establish communication with family members. When you are satisfied that your family is all right, stay off the phone. There are probably people in situations more serious than yours, and they may need to call for help. Keep the phone lines clear for such emergencies.

A serious emergency is one in which your life or someone else's life is in danger. Being frightened by the sudden dark is not a life-threatening emergency. Do not call 911. Instead, find the battery-powered radio in your emergency kit. Listen to the radio for information on what is happening and what you can do.

You may also need the flashlight in your emergency kit. Even if the power outage occurs during the day, it could continue into the night. Have emergency lighting handy. Remember the American Red Cross warning about emergency lighting: never use candles!

Resist the temptation to go to the refrigerator for a soda or some ice. Every time the door to the freezer or refrigerator is opened, cold air escapes and warmer air enters. Keeping the doors closed keeps the food inside safer for a longer period of time.

But if the power remains off for more than two hours, the perishable food in your refrigerator is in danger of spoiling. The food in your freezer should be safe for one to two days. After two hours, you should protect your spoil-able refrigerated foods. Put them in ice chests and pack ice—perhaps the ice blocks you have already prepared in your freezer—around them. The ice chests do not have to be expensive—styrofoam coolers do a good job. The ice will keep the foods better than a refrigerator that is begin-ning to warm up.

No matter how long the power disruption lasts, do not travel unless absolutely necessary. When traffic lights are out, cars slow down (as they should) and streets become clogged with the slowing vehicles. Drivers can be confused and accidents can result. Also, people may become irritated with the delays and they may not drive courteously. If you

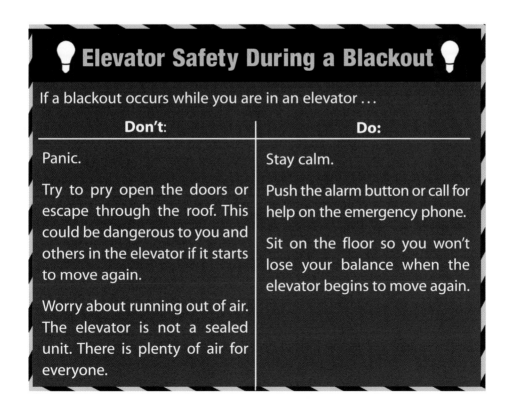

## 💡 Elevator Safety During a Blackout 💡

If a blackout occurs while you are in an elevator ...

| Don't: | Do: |
| --- | --- |
| Panic. | Stay calm. |
| Try to pry open the doors or escape through the roof. This could be dangerous to you and others in the elevator if it starts to move again. | Push the alarm button or call for help on the emergency phone.<br><br>Sit on the floor so you won't lose your balance when the elevator begins to move again. |
| Worry about running out of air. The elevator is not a sealed unit. There is plenty of air for everyone. | |

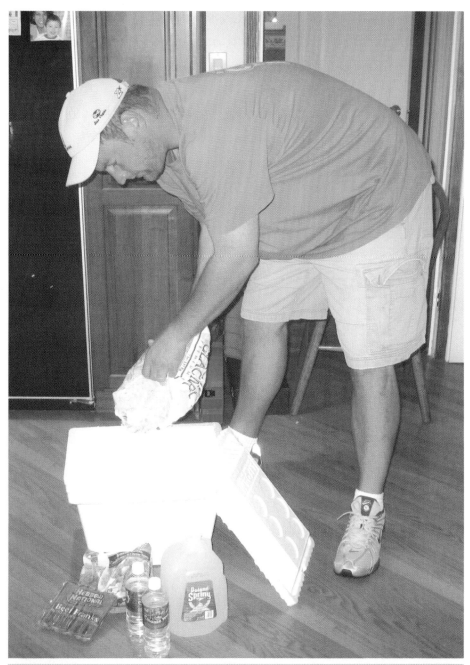

You don't have to spend a lot of money to store perishable foods during a blackout. Simply have an inexpensive styrofoam cooler on hand. If it looks like the blackout may last more than two hours, pack your dairy products, meats, leftovers, and other perishable items in the cooler and surround them with ice.

must go somewhere, it is important to drive especially carefully. Treat every intersection as if it is a four-way stop: stop completely, look carefully, and go through only if you are sure no cars will hit yours.

# Using a Generator

Some homes have generators to protect against power outages. Generators use gas engines to produce electricity. If you have a generator, you need to watch out for three dangers: toxic exhaust, electrocution, and fire.

The gas engines in generators, like those in cars, emit carbon monoxide. You cannot see or smell this gas, but it is deadly. It is, therefore, extremely important that generators not be operated in closed spaces. They should never be operated in garages or basements. They should not even be run in partially closed spaces such as carports. They must always be outdoors.

If you are using a generator, keep it far away from your house's windows, doors, and vents. The gas can come inside through these openings. A carbon monoxide detector will let you know if the toxic gas is in your home. That is, if the detector is battery-operated and the batteries are good.

The second danger of generators is electrocution. The generator makes electricity, and sometimes that electricity can "leak," unseen, through the metal wall of the generator. Any moisture on or around the generator can cause people nearby to be electrocuted by the "leaking" electricity. If you are using a generator to supply power, make sure it is dry and you are dry.

A generator can produce a lot of electricity. You might be tempted to connect it to an outlet in your house and plug several appliances in to the same outlet. Don't do it! When the power comes back on, your electricity will be going from the generator to the outlet to the transmission lines. This is called backfeeding into the power lines. The extra surge from your generator could shock or electrocute someone working on the lines. Instead, plug only the appliances you need directly into the generator.

The third danger from generators is setting a fire. When generators are running, they get hot. That heat can spark a fire. When the generator runs low on fuel, it needs more gas. But if any gasoline spills on a hot generator, it can burst into flames. If you need to refuel a generator, turn it off first and give it plenty of time to cool.

## Keeping Warm or Cool

Power outages can be most serious when they occur on extremely cold or terribly hot days. Because people tend to use more energy on those days, blackouts are more likely to happen then. If the power goes out when it is very cold, bundle up as best you can. Several layers of clothing will keep you warmer than one heavy coat or blanket. Moving around will help, too. Exercising raises your body's temperature.

Keeping cool during a summer blackout is a little harder. One of the most obvious ways is to wear light clothing. Clothing should be light in weight and light in color. Darker colors absorb heat, and light colors reflect heat.

Stay inside, out of the sun. If you live in a house or apartment with access to several stories, stay on the first floor or, better yet, in a basement below ground. Heat rises, so lower floors are cooler than higher ones.

Just as moving around helps you stay warm, not moving much will help keep you cool. Taking a cool shower or bath would be nice, but it is not a good idea. Remember, water is pumped to your faucets by electricity. Most city water systems will have water for a while, but in an extended blackout that water supply will run out. Save the water for drinking.

Drinking water is the best thing you can do to stay cool. Other liquids do not keep you as cool as water does. Some, such as those with alcohol and caffeine, actually raise your body temperature. Don't forget your pets. Make sure they have plenty of food and water, too.

If you follow these suggestions, you can most likely get through the hottest summer blackout or the coldest winter power outage. Now you need to know what to do when the lights come back on.

# 4 --- When the Lights Are Back On

**E**very disaster leaves destruction in its wake. Floods, hurricanes, mudslides—they all end in property damage and heartache. Major blackouts are no exception. The City Council of New York estimated that the 2003 power outage cost the city more than a half billion dollars. Most of this damage, however, was to businesses and the government. When stores cannot operate, restaurants cannot cook food, and theaters must close. Those businesses lose money. Power company workers, policemen, firemen, traffic controllers, and other emergency workers must be paid to work overtime.

For most families, however, blackouts are usually just inconveniences. Unless they trigger widespread crime, as the New York City blackout of 1977 did, power outages do not cause many injuries. People who are prepared and follow the recommended precautions generally come out of a blackout—even a prolonged one—with little difficulty.

We have discussed preparation and the precautions to take during a blackout. Now we need to look at what to do when the blackout ends.

## Immediately After

If you have followed the guidelines carefully, you will know the blackout is over when the one light you left on lights up. You may also hear noises coming from your refrigerator.

A police officer leads passengers on the subway tracks to the nearest station in New York City after the North American blackout. More than 400,000 passengers on 600 subway and railroad cars stuck between stations had to be evacuated that day. Fortunately, this was carried out with no serious injuries.

Wait a few minutes before you do anything. If you turn all your appliances on right away, you will increase the demand on the system that was just restored. If lots of people did that, the sudden heavy demand could make the system go out again. First, turn your heater on (or air conditioner if it is summer). Then wait ten or fifteen minutes and connect only the appliances you need.

Once you know that everyone is safe, your equipment is working, and there is no danger from fires, you can turn your attention to the important matters of food and drink. After a long power outage, the food in your refrigerator and the water in your faucet may not be safe to consume.

# Safe Water

Systems that purify water usually rely on electricity. These systems may not be working in a prolonged blackout. When the power is restored, it may take time for purified water to be available. The Centers for Disease Control and Prevention recommends that people contact their local or state health department after a blackout to find out if their water is safe for drinking. If it is not, the health department will explain how to treat the water to make it safe.

The water in this glass pan has been brought to a rapid, rolling boil. This rolling boil should continue for at least one minute. Be sure you can easily lift the pot without spilling the water once it has boiled. If small children are around, boil the water on a back burner, out of reach.

The most effective way to purify water is to boil it. Put the water in a pot and heat it until the top of the water bubbles. This is called a rolling boil. Keep the water boiling for a full minute. Boiling for one minute kills most harmful organisms. Properly boiled water and bottled water are safe to drink.

If water is not safe to drink, it is not safe for most other household uses. Do not use untreated water to wash your hands, your food, or your dishes. Do not use it to brush your teeth.

This dairy section of a grocery store has been marked off after a blackout to alert customers that these products will be discarded. Dairy products that have been at room temperature for too long are at risk of bacterial contamination, which could lead to serious illness if consumed.

# Safe Food

Next to water safety, food safety is the most serious issue following a lengthy power outage. If you kept your refrigerator and freezer closed during the blackout, and the blackout lasted less than two hours, you do not need to worry. After two hours, however, most refrigerators have lost enough coolness that the food in them begins to spoil.

Foods in the freezer will stay safe longer. A full freezer keeps food safe for forty-eight hours. In a half-full freezer, food will keep for twenty-four hours.

How can you tell if your food is safe to eat? One way is to check it with a digital quick-response thermometer (an item you may want to keep in your emergency kit). If a perishable food item registers higher than 40 degrees Fahrenheit (4 degrees Celsius) and has been kept at that temperature for more than two hours, it is probably not safe. Exceptions are butter, hard cheeses, opened cans or bottles of fruit and fruit juices, breads, salad dressings, jellies, and bottled sauces. You can keep these items, but throw away everything else that was warmer than 40°F (4°C) for more than two hours.

Foods in the freezer are safe even if they have begun to thaw, as long as they have ice crystals on them and the temperature in the freezer is 40°F (4°C) or below. They should either be cooked right away or refrozen. Even if items have started to thaw, partially thawed food can be refrozen. The food loses some of its taste quality, but it is perfectly safe. Any once-frozen food that has been kept above 40°F (4°C) for longer than two hours should be thrown away. Remember,

Seafood, eggs, and pizza are considered unsafe to eat if they have gone for more than two hours without refrigeration. If you want to keep them safe, pack them in your iced cooler.

# A FOOD SAFETY CHECKLIST

**Remember!**

💡 Never taste a food to find out if it has spoiled. When in doubt, throw it out!

💡 Discard all spoiled foods in plastic bags or containers that can be well tied or sealed.

💡 Perishable foods that are unsafe after two hours without refrigeration:

chicken, seafood, red meat, bacon, hot dogs, opened cans of meat, eggs or egg dishes, milk, yogurt, soft cheese, opened containers of mayonnaise, creamy salad dressings, pizza, pasta, pasta salads, rolls, biscuits, potato salads, opened containers of tomato sauce, cooked vegetables, cream-filled pastries, cookie dough, freshly cut fruits

💡 Once-frozen foods that can be refrozen if they are only partially thawed:

raw meats (including beef, veal, chicken, and ground meats), seafood, eggs and egg products, hard and soft cheeses, fruits, juices, cakes, pies, pastries, corn meal, flour, vegetables, frozen meals, casseroles

*(continued on following page)*

## A FOOD SAFETY CHECKLIST

*(continued from previous page)*

💡 Foods that can be kept for a limited time without refrigeration:

butter, margarine, hard cheeses, opened cans of fruit and fruit juices, vinegar-based salad dressings, raw vegetables, jelly, herbs, waffles, pancakes, pies

when in doubt about a food being safe to eat, it is better to throw it out than to risk it being spoiled!

If you have been away from home during the power disruption, you may not know how long your food has been at what temperature. Your food could have thawed and refrozen. It may or may not be safe. One way you can tell is to keep a bag or other container of ice cubes in your freezer. If the cubes look like they melted and froze

The casserole and red meat above may still be safe to eat if they were frozen and were only beginning to thaw. Fruits, vegetables, and bread can remain longer at room temperature.

again in one blob, it is best to throw the food in the freezer away.

# Returning to Normal

For many people who live through a serious blackout, throwing out spoiled or unsafe food is the greatest expense. Some lose money because they cannot work at their jobs without electricity. But after the event is over, their lives return to normal.

People who are trapped in elevators or trains or are far from home when the lights go out may suffer hardship. Others who are in accidents or who stumble in the dark get hurt. Those who are caught in darkened stairways or unfamiliar parts of towns may be frightened. But before long, their lives, too, go back to normal.

Sometimes when everything is smooth and there are no emergencies, we forget that we always need to be prepared in case another problem occurs. Once life has returned to normal, be sure to check your emergency supply kit and restock it if you used anything. Go over the emergency communication plan with your family again. Make sure everyone knows the numbers to call. Review the "Preparing for a Blackout" checklist and follow its guidelines. That way, you will be ready if another one occurs.

One thing a blackout does for many people is remind them how much they depend on electricity. And it shows them that they can get along, even if only for a few hours, without it. A blackout makes many people determined to figure out ways to conserve all the energy they can.

# 5 --- Preventing Blackouts

**A**fter every major blackout, energy experts discuss how to prevent the next one. Some say we need to build more power plants for our growing demand. More power plants and more transmission cables would mean more electricity would be available. But power plants are very expensive to build. Building them would make electricity cost much more, and people do not want to pay more for their power.

Many power disruptions are caused by old and failing equipment. The great Northeast blackout of 1965 began when one small piece of equipment, a relay, did not work properly. It caused a single transmission line to disconnect from the system, and that made others overload and disconnect. Within two and a half seconds, the failures had cascaded throughout the entire Northeast. Some people want power companies to invest more money in better cables and equipment. Others point out that even $100 million in system upgrades will not fix everything that needs improving.

Some energy experts suggest that the government should regulate the utility business more. They point out that all the different companies have different standards and different practices. If one group—the government—had more control, they argue, every power company would have to follow the same rules. They could be forced to do things like trim trees around power lines. The 2003 North

American blackout was triggered when transmission cables sagged into trees. Still, many people think that government regulation would only make things worse.

All the energy experts agree on one thing: conserving energy can reduce the number of blackouts. Cutting back on energy use reduces demand. Every blackout, whatever the trigger, occurred when demand exceeded supply.

You can conserve energy in two ways. You can be careful not to waste any, and you can make sure that your appliances operate efficiently.

Power from power plants is transmitted to consumers through overhead power transmission lines, as pictured here, or underground cables. The steel lattice-work transmission towers support the high-voltage lines. Voltage is lowered to the current needed by homes and offices once it reaches the power substations. Overhead power lines sagging in trees are blamed for the 2003 Northeast blackout.

# Reducing Energy Waste

The biggest energy use in your home is heating and cooling. You can save energy by making sure none of the valuable heat or coolness is lost in your house or apartment. One way to keep the warmed or cooled air in is to insulate your house. Putting insulation in the ceilings, attic, walls, floors, and crawl spaces of your house is like wrapping yourself in a protective coat. You can make that coat tighter by putting weather stripping around doors and windows. If you live in an apartment and are concerned that the building's insulation may be inadequate, bring it to the attention of the building owner or landlord. You may be able to install weather stripping to prevent drafts around the doors and windows of your apartment, however.

Insulated blankets also keep the heat in water heaters from being wasted.

If there are any holes or cracks in the walls or around windows, doors, fixtures, and electrical switches and outlets, warm or cool air can leak out. Caulking those cracks saves energy.

Any opening to the outside can allow air to escape. Open fireplace dampers send the air in a house right up the chimney. Ventilating fans, usually used in the kitchen and bathrooms to pull odors out, also pull air outside. Be sure to turn them off when they are not needed.

If some of the rooms in your home are not used very much, do not waste energy heating or cooling them. Close the door to the room and turn off the heating or cooling to that room.

Here, fiberglass insulation is being installed in the roof of a home that is being built. Insulation provides a resistance to the flow of heat that naturally occurs from a warmer to a cooler space. Insulation keeps a consistent temperature throughout a home, making it warmer in the winter and keeping the cool air inside during the summer.

Sometimes energy is wasted by keeping the house or apartment warmer or cooler than needed. In the winter, the thermostat should be set no higher than 68°F (20°C). In the summer, it should be no lower than 78°F (26°C). Setting your house or apartment temperature carefully is probably the best way to conserve energy.

There are many ways energy is being wasted in the photo above. Overhead lights are on during the daytime, doors are left open, allowing cool (or warm) air to escape outside, and a television is on with no one watching it. By turning appliances and lights off when not in use and closing doors to the outside, you can save energy and thus decrease the chance of blackouts.

On sunny days, do not waste the solar energy that is free. In cold weather, keep the draperies, blinds, or shades open during the day, especially on your south-facing windows, to allow the sun's warmth in. Keep the windows clean so dirt is not blocking the sun's rays. At night and in the hot summer, when you do not want the outside heat to come inside, close the window coverings. If the window coverings are white, they will reflect heat away from the house or apartment.

Also, clean the dirt and dust from radiators and other heating units. Be sure to remove air-conditioner units from windows during winter.

After heating and cooling, the next biggest home energy use is lighting and other appliances. Here, too, people waste energy. How

## A QUICK LIST OF NO- AND LOW-COST IDEAS TO SAVE ENERGY!

These recommendations from the U.S. Department of Energy can help you and your family save energy and money at home.

- Take showers instead of baths.
- Wash only full loads of dishes and clothes.
- Drip-dry dishes instead of using the dishwasher's drying cycle.
- Replace incandescent lightbulbs with compact fluorescent lamps.
- Turn off your computer and monitor when not in use.
- Plug your home electronics (such as televisions and VCRs) into power strips. Turn off the strips when the electronics are not in use.
- Use your microwave rather than your conventional stove or oven.
- Lower the thermostat on your hot water heater. The U.S. Department of Energy suggests 115°F (46°C).

Source: http://www.eere.energy.gov/consumerinfo/saveenergy/save_nocost.html

often do you leave lights, televisions, fans, stereos, and other appliances on when no one is using them? Any time something electric is on and not being used, energy is wasted. Dimmers, timers, and motion sensors can be used to help you keep unused appliances off.

A big offender in the wasted energy category is the home computer. Computer manufacturers used to advise people to leave their machines on all the time. When computers were fairly new, turning them off and on may have damaged them. That is no longer the case. The computer, its monitor, printer, and other accessories should be turned off when not in use.

Energy is wasted when you use power you do not need. Do you really need your electric dishwasher to dry your dishes? Why not turn the power off, open the door, and let them air dry instead? Can you wash your clothes in warm or cold water instead of hot? That would save the electricity it takes to heat the water.

## Using Appliances Efficiently

Another way people waste energy is by not using their appliances as efficiently as possible. They use big appliances to do little jobs. When you wash clothes, for example, do you wait until you have a full load? It takes just as much electricity to run the washer for a full load as for a partial load. The same is true for a dishwasher. Some appliances have settings for small and large loads, but you save the most energy when the machine is full.

The same principle applies to lighting. Don't use a big lightbulb when a smaller one will do. Match the wattage

## Heat Loss from a House

A picture is worth..., in this case, lost heating dollars. This thermal photograph shows heat leaking from a house during those expensive winter heating months. The white, yellow, and red colors show where the heat escapes, with the red representing the area of the greatest heat loss.

Thermo

Normal

Thermogram/photograph copyright 1997, Infraspection Institute, Inc., Shelburne, VT

COOL ████████████████████ HOT

This dramatic image is posted on the U.S. Department of Energy's Web site. It shows how heat energy is escaping a home during the winter. Notice the heat leaking from the ground and roof as well as from the front of the house. Making home improvements such as installing insulation and weather stripping can make this home more energy efficient.

of the bulb to the amount of light you need. Reading or working might require a brighter bulb than watching television or talking. Also, a single 75-watt bulb is better than two 40- or 60-watt bulbs. It takes less energy and gives more light.

Matching the size of the chore to the size of the appliance applies to cooking tasks, too. Use large appliances for large jobs, and small ones for small jobs. To cook a big meal or several items at once, use the oven. For smaller quantities, use the stovetop, electric pans, a toaster, or a toaster oven. On the stovetop, fit the pan to the burner. Heating a large burner and using a pan too small to cover the burner wastes energy. Using a small pan on a large burner wastes all the energy of the part of the burner not covered by the pan.

Is there one room in your home where it seems everyone forgets to turn off the light? Make a sticker or a sign reminding your family members not to forget. Always turn off the light when leaving a room, even if only for a few minutes.

Electric burners and ovens take a few minutes to cool down after they are turned off. Do not waste this heat energy. Turn the stove or oven off a few minutes before your food is done. The food will stay hot long enough to continue cooking.

Use a pressure cooker or a microwave whenever you can. They are not only smaller than most ovens, but they also save energy by cutting down on the amount of time food has to cook. Another simple way to reduce cooking time—and, therefore, conserve energy—is to put lids on the pans on your stove. Water will boil faster when it is covered.

As strange as it may sound, water will also boil faster when the stovetop is clean. Clean burners and reflectors hold and reflect heat better and thus save energy. In fact, keeping your appliances clean and properly maintained are two of the best ways to ensure that they operate at maximum efficiency.

Filters on furnaces and air conditioners get dirty. When they do, the appliance has to force its warm or cool air through the screen of dirt. The dirtier the filter, the harder the appliance has to work to maintain the same temperature. The harder the appliance must work, the more electricity it uses. Clean or replace filters regularly, usually once a month during the heating and cooling seasons.

Other appliances also have filters. Dryers have lint traps, and some vacuums have filters. Keeping the working parts of your appliances clean keeps them efficient.

Some appliances are more efficient than others. An evaporative cooler (swamp cooler), for example, uses far less electricity than an air conditioner. So do fans. Fluorescent lamps use less energy than incandescent lightbulbs. Newer refrigerators, dishwashers, and washing

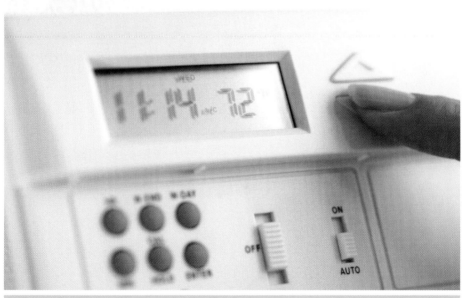

A digital thermostat monitor is a great energy-saving device for a home. Unlike mechanical thermostats, digital thermostats can be programmed to automatically turn air conditioning and heat on and off throughout the day, depending on when it is needed. This helps to avoid running it when no one is home.

machines and dryers often are more energy efficient than older ones. To conserve energy, use the most efficient appliances you can that will do the job you need done.

You may wonder if conserving energy makes any difference. Can changing your thermostat, turning off lights, or using a toaster oven really help prevent blackouts? The answer is yes. If everyone saved just a little, demand would go down and supply would go up.

Conservation can reduce the number of power outages, but future blackouts are still likely. Energy experts say that we will almost certainly face more blackouts as we continue to depend on electricity. What we need, the experts say, is to know how to cope with them. We need to be prepared.

# Glossary

**American Sign Language (ASL)** The language of articulated hand gestures used primarily by the hearing impaired. It is the dominant sign language in the United States, English-speaking parts of Canada, and some parts of Mexico.

**backfeed** Flow of electric power from an appliance or equipment back to the transmission line.

**braille** A system of writing for the blind that is made up of raised dots. A blind person reads by touching the characters with his or her fingers.

**brownout** A reduction in the voltage of electricity supplied to an area.

**carbon monoxide** A colorless, odorless, poisonous gas that results when carbon is burned with insufficient air.

**cascade** Rippling effect of several parts of a power grid failing, one after another; a cascading blackout occurs when several parts of a power grid fail.

**caulk** An elastic material used to seal cracks and crevices to stop leaking.

**damper** In a fireplace, a movable iron plate that regulates the draft and allows smoke to flow up the chimney.

**electrocution** Death caused by an electric current flowing through the body.

**evaporative cooler**  A type of cooling unit that saturates the air with water vapor, in turn cooling the air. It is also called a swamp cooler and is most often used in warm, dry climates.

**fluorescent lamp**  A type of electric lamp that has a coating of phosphor, a fluorescent material, that then converts ultraviolet energy into light. This type of lamp is considered more efficient than incandescent light-bulbs because it converts more energy to light rather than heat.

**generator**  A portable device that uses gasoline to produce electricity.

**grid**  A network of power plants, transmission stations, and transmission lines that produces and deliver electrical power.

**ignition**  The action or means by which the burning of fuel is started.

**incandescent**  A bright light that glows with intense heat. An incandescent bulb has a filament that gives off light when heated.

**insulate**  To isolate or set apart so as to prevent energy loss.

**manually**  By hand; without the use of a machine.

**perishable**  Liable to spoil or decay.

**pressure cooker**  An airtight cooking pot in which food can be cooked using pressurized steam.

**reflector**  A polished surface that reflects light.

**respirator**  A device that is used to assist with breathing or to maintain artificial breathing.

**rolling blackout**  A controlled power outage in which power is shut off to selected areas for limited periods of time.

**rolling boil** Condition of a liquid when it is heated to the point at which large bubbles form at the surface.

**surge** A sudden rise of electrical current. A rush or forceful flow.

**toxic** Poisonous.

**tram** A streetcar that runs on rails and is powered by electricity.

**transmission cable** Conductor that distributes electric current from a power plant to consumers.

**utility** A public service, such as gas, water, or electricity.

**ventilator** A breathing machine, also known as a respirator.

**voltage** The force that causes electricity to flow; electric potential, measured in volts.

**wattage** Amount of electric power, measured in watts.

**weather stripping** A strip of material that can be installed around doors and windows that prevents drafts of air or moisture.

# For More Information

American Red Cross National Headquarters
2025 E Street, NW
Washington, DC 20006
(202) 303-4498
Disaster Assistance: (866) GET-INFO (866-438-4636)
Web site: http://www.redcross.org

Federal Emergency Management Agency (FEMA)
500 C Street, SW
Washington, DC 20472
(202) 566-1600
Web site: http://www.fema.gov

## Web Sites

Due to the changing nature of Internet links, the Rosen Publishing Group, Inc., has developed an online list of Web sites related to the subject of this book. This site is updated regularly. Please use the link below to access the list:

http://www.rosenlinks.com/lep/blac

# For Further Reading

De Angelis, Therese. *Blackout!: Cities in Darkness*. Berkeley Heights, NJ: Enslow, 2003.

Goodman, James. *Blackout*. New York, NY: North Point Press, 2003.

Grossman, Peter Z. *In Came the Darkness: The Story of Blackouts*. New York, NY: Simon and Schuster, 1984.

Weiner, Eric. *Blackout!* (Ghostwriter). New York, NY: Skylark, 1993.

# Bibliography

Apt, Jay, and Lester B. Lave. "Blackouts Are Inevitable." *Washington Post*, August 10, 2004, p. A19.

The Blackout History Project. Retrieved May 5, 2005 (http://blackout.gmu.edu/).

Centers for Disease Control and Prevention. "Public Health Issues Related to Summertime Blackouts." Retrieved May 5, 2005 (http://www.bt.cdc.gov/poweroutage/blackout.asp).

CNN.com. "Power Returns to Most Areas Hit by Blackout." August 15, 2003. Retrieved on May 5, 2005 (http://www.cnn.com/2003/US/08/15/power.outage/index.html).

CNN.com. "Sagging Power Lines, Hot Weather Blamed for Blackout." August 11, 1996. Retrieved May 5, 2005 (http://www.cnn.com/US/9608/11/power.outage/).

Langfield, Amy. "Amy Langfield's New York Notebook." August 15, 2003. Retrieved January 11, 2005 (http://amylangfield.com/2003_08_10_archive.html).

Manor, Robert. "The 2003 Blackout: Fallout and Lessons," *Chicago Tribune*, August 8, 2004.

Pacific Gas and Electric Company. "Power Outage Safety." Retrieved on May 5, 2005 (http://pge.com/safety/prepare_natural_disasters/emergency_preparedness/plans/outage_safety.html).

U.S. Department of Energy, Office of Energy Efficiency
and Renewable Energy. "Your Home's Energy Use."
Retrieved on May 5, 2005 (http://www.eere.energy.gov/
consumerinfo/energy_savers/energyuse.html).

# Index

## About the Author

Ann Byers is a California educator and youth worker. While researching this book, she recalled the vivid, eye-witness accounts she heard from ordinary citizens who were affected by the 1965 Northeast blackout and 1977 New York City blackout. As a California resident, she has been a "victim" of brownouts and numerous rolling blackouts. While at a conference in Palm Springs, California, she experienced firsthand the discomforts, uncertainty, and inconveniences of the West Coast blackout in the summer of 1996.

## Photo Credits

Cover, pp. 1, 5, 6, 8, 10, 18, 37, 39 © AP/Wide World Photos; p. 11 © Bettmann/Corbis; pp. 14, 51 courtesy of the United States Department of Energy; pp. 15, 32, 48 by Tahara Anderson; p. 20 © Howard Sokol/Index Stock; p. 21 © Chuck Savage/Corbis; p. 23 © Dorothy Litell Greco/The Image Works; p. 25 © Shelly Harrison/Index Stock; p. 26 © David Aubrey/Corbis; p. 29 © Monika Graff/The Image Works; p. 38 © Daniel E. Way/The Image Works; pp. 41 (top and center), 42 (third and fourth images) © Photodisc/2004 Punchstock; pp. 41 (bottom), 53 © Royalty-Free/Corbis; p. 42 (top) © Klaus Stemmier/Corbis; p. 42 (second image) © Rick Gayle Studio/Corbis; p. 45 © John Henley/Corbis; p. 47 © James L. Amos/Corbis; p. 52 © Ed Brock/Corbis.

Designer: Tahara Anderson
Editor: Leigh Ann Cobb